Voting With a Porpoise

By

Russell Glass and Sean Callahan

Illustrated by

Daniel Howarth

Voting with a Porpoise

Published by
Books with a Porpoise
Menlo Park, CA

Hardcover ISBN: 978-1-7327454-0-7
Paperback ISBN: 978-1-7327454-1-4
eISBN: 978-1-7327454-2-1

Illustrations by: Daniel Howarth
Interior Design: GKS Creative
Project Management: The Cadence Group

The authors created this book to help change the culture around elections and voting. To that end, 100 percent of the profits for *Voting with a Porpoise* will be donated to 501(c)(3) non-partisan voting-related causes focused on getting more people of all backgrounds to the polls, such as Rock the Vote, Vote.org, TurboVote, and others.

Library of Congress Information is on file with the Publisher.

For my wonderful pod:
Robin, Ava, Mackenzie, and Annika.
~ Russ

For Nancy, Sophie, Charlotte, Marty Musker,
and sea mammals everywhere.
~ Sean

Once upon a time
a dolphin pod played
and happily ate fish
in the reef where they stayed.

But one day, the fish they ate left the reef.
The ocean had warmed,
and they needed relief.

Now the whole dolphin pod
was as hungry as can be.
Even Petey, the small porpoise,
had to agree.

Finn's stomach
was rumbling.
"I'm hungry," he said.

We need to eat soon,
Mimi thought
in her head.

The pod had to choose
to go or to stay.
Finn said, “I’m the leader,
and we stay, I say.”

"Finn, not fair!" said Mimi.
"That's not only your call.
This choice is important
and should be made by us all."

"I have an idea!"
Petey loudly called.
"We should have an election
to decide for us all."

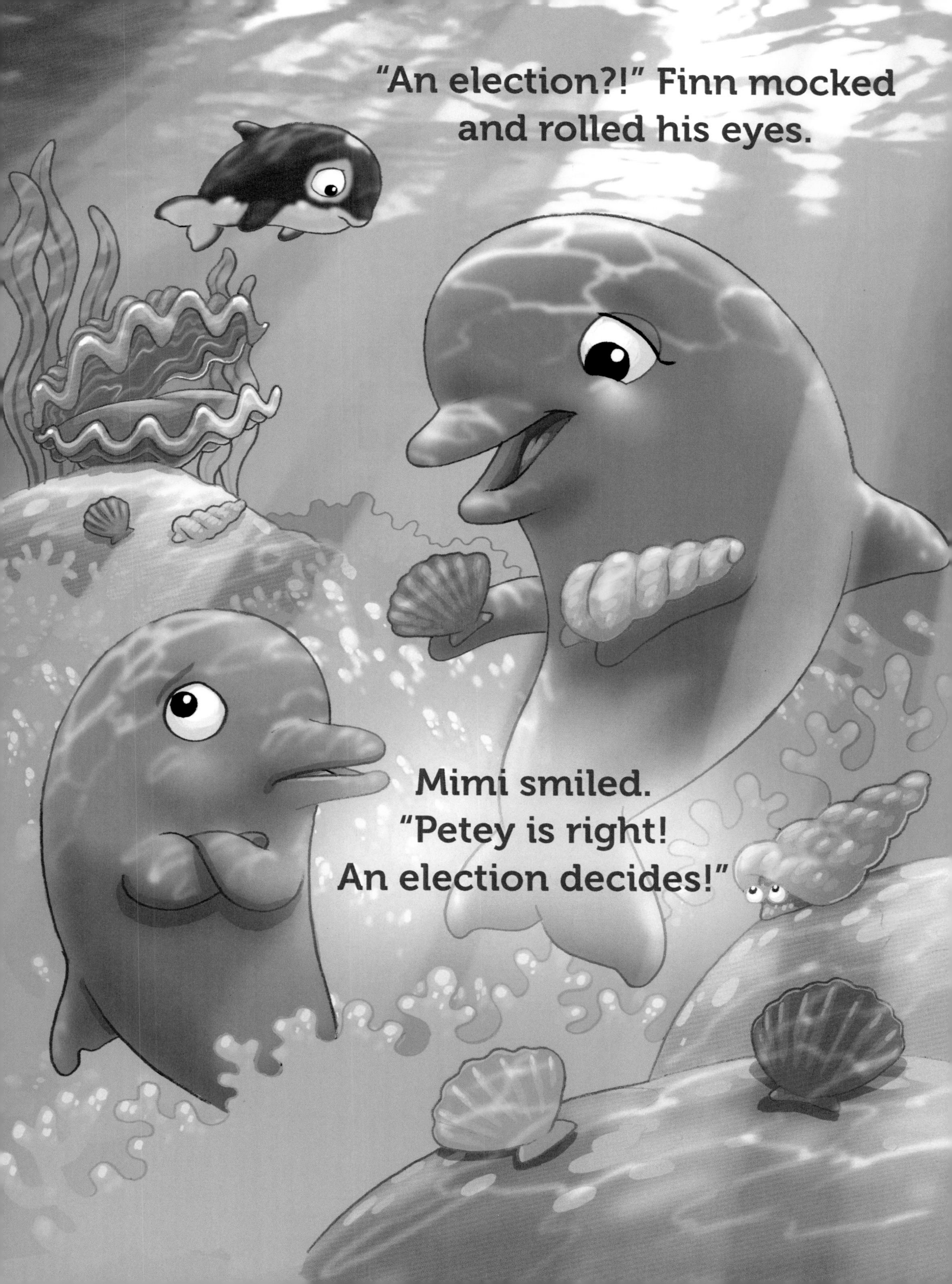

"An election?!" Finn mocked and rolled his eyes.

Mimi smiled. "Petey is right! An election decides!"

"We all could vote
and the most votes
would win!"
"I guess that
sounds fair,"
softly grumbled Finn.

Five votes for leaving
and five for staying.
"But wait, we are eleven,"
Mimi counted, while saying,

"Petey, why didn't you vote?
You are one of us."
"He can't vote," said Finn.
"He's just a porpoise!"

Mimi shouted,
"Finn, again, that's not at all fair!
Petey's in our pod.
Voting's his right to share."

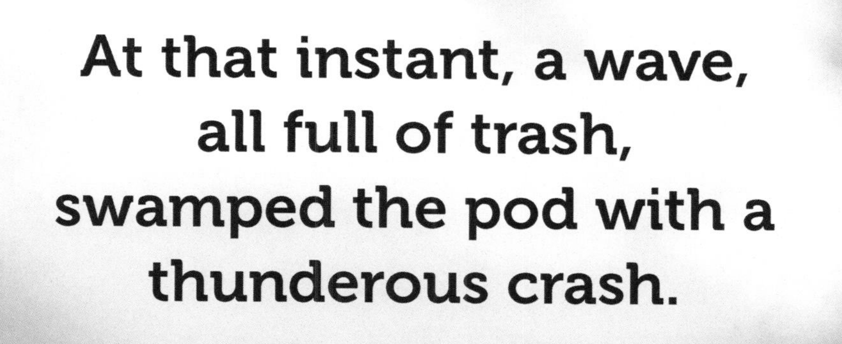

At that instant, a wave,
all full of trash,
swamped the pod with a
thunderous crash.

A six-pack ring
landed on Finn's beak
and tied it shut tight.
He started to shriek!

The pod watched in shock,
too frightened to see.
But Petey dove quick
to help Finn get free.

He grabbed with his teeth
and pulled with full might.
Then POP! went the ring
and ended Finn's plight.

Finn thanked Petey
for saving him today
and didn't fuss when
Petey voted, "Let's swim away!"

"That decides it," said Mimi.
"We have voted to go."
So they swam and swam,
though tired and slow.

Then, after four days,
when the sun started to rise,
Mimi saw hundreds
of birds in the skies.

"FISH!!" she shouted
and she was quite right.
The birds had millions
of fish in their sight.

The dolphins swam fast and jumped in and out,
eating and laughing and spraying their spouts.

They had found a home
where they could survive.
Finn said, "The election
kept us alive!"

"Mimi, we should elect you
as our new pod leader!"
Then they voted again as
the whole pod cheered her!

Why is voting important?

To the parents and other adults who are reading this book: Voting is how we solve problems, make decisions, and hold our politicians accountable. In the United States, however, democracy isn't currently working as it was designed. That's because too many people aren't voting. That's a big problem, because government has to pay attention only to those who show up at the polls or those with money to fund turnout efforts. Democracy works as designed only when citizens participate and vote.

**The fix is easy:
We all need to be voters and
we all need to show up on election day.**

If we were all voters, then divisive, self-serving, and obstructionist politicians would be swept away and the good ones (like Mimi!) would serve the people.

Like it is supposed to work.

And when that happens, we can aim the world's most powerful economy and idea engine at creating opportunities for everyone.

Our hope is that you can use *Voting with a Porpoise* to help your children and their friends begin to understand how important it is to participate in holding politicians accountable and crafting the nation they want to live in.

We created this book to help change the culture around elections and voting. To that end, 100 percent of the profits for *Voting with a Porpoise* will be donated to 501(c)(3) nonpartisan voting-related causes focused on getting more people of all backgrounds to the polls, such as Rock the Vote, Vote.org, TurboVote, and others. Learn more and order merch to support the cause at www.bookswithaporpoise.com.

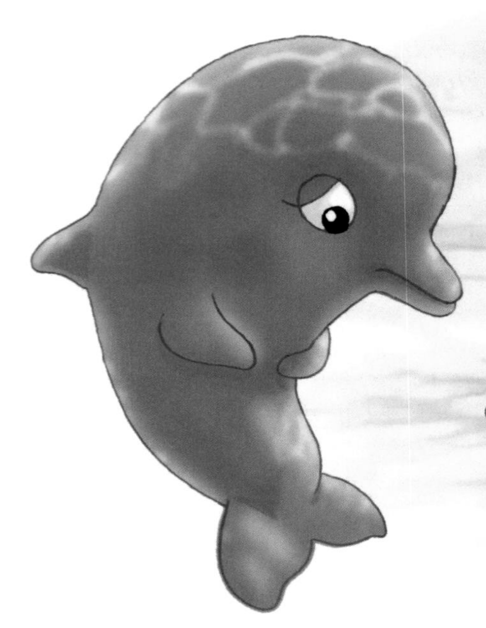

What is the difference between a dolphin and a porpoise?

Dolphins and porpoises are both in the order Cetacea, which comes from the Greek word *ketos* (large sea creature). Whales are also part of this order.

Dolphins and porpoises have many similarities, one of which is their extreme intelligence. Both have large, complex brains and a structure in their foreheads called the melon, with which they generate sonar (sound waves) to better navigate their underwater world.

Dolphins tend to have prominent, elongated "beaks," while porpoises have smaller mouths and teeth. The dolphin's hooked or curved dorsal fin (the one in the middle of the animal's back) also differs from the porpoise's triangular dorsal fin. Dolphin bodies tend to be leaner and larger than porpoises and their coloring lighter. Dolphins are usually more social and talkative than porpoises and live in larger groups called pods. Source: NOAA.Gov

Conversation Starters and Lesson Ideas

- Ask children to vote on their choices of snack—one mark for each snack on the list. All the children get to eat the choice with the most votes.
- Ask children to give ideas on what else the dolphin pod could vote on as a group to help them get settled in their new home.
- Ask children if they think they should be able to vote for something that isn't in the option set.
- Talk to children about integrity of the voting process—for example, would it be fair if any child was able to vote more than once?
- Talk to children about how they should vote if they don't like any of the choices.
- Talk to children about fairness—for example, as them to discuss whether only children who ar able to climb on the monkey bars should be abl to vote or whether it should be open to everyon
- Talk to children about what happens if they ar on the losing side of the vote.
- Talk to children about using their voice to expres their opinions.
- Talk to children about courage and doing thing that might feel scary at first.
- Talk to children about the environment, wha climate change means, and how recycling is a important activity to keep the oceans clean.

About the Authors

RUSSELL GLASS is a serial technology entrepreneur and author, having founded or held senior positions at five venture-backed technology companies and writing *The Big Data-Driven Business*. He is currently the CEO of Ginger.io, a company providing instant behavioral health support whenever and wherever needed. He sold his last company, Bizo, to LinkedIn, where he ran the Marketing Solutions products group. Since leaving LinkedIn in 2017, Russ joined the board of Rock the Vote and has been focused on using his experience with technology, data science, and narrative/branding tactics to develop novel strategies to increase engagement and turnout among young voters.

SEAN CALLAHAN is a content marketer at LinkedIn. He has written several previous books, including *The Big Data-Driven Business*, *The Leprechaun Who Lost His Rainbow*, and *A Wild Father's Day*. A former reporter, his freelance journalism has appeared in *The New York Times, The Washington Post,* and *Notre Dame Magazine*. He lives with his wife and two daughters in Chicago. He's also a voter.

About the Illustrator

DANIEL HOWARTH is a freelance graphic designer and illustrator. He has illustrated dozens of children's books, including *I Love You, Grandpa* and *A Wild Father's Day*. He lives near Exeter with his wife and family and is a cofounder of How On Earth, a vegan food company.

Made in the USA
Lexington, KY
13 February 2019